A DARK DARK TALE

For William, Edward and Alice Cowling

First published in the United States 1981
by Dial Books for Young Readers
A Division of NAL Penguin Inc.
2 Park Avenue
New York, New York 10016

Published in Great Britain
by Andersen Press Ltd.
Copyright © 1981 by Ruth Brown
All rights reserved.
Library of Congress Catalog Card Number: 81-66798
First Pied Piper Printing 1984
Printed in Hong Kong by South China Printing Co.
COBE
10 9 8 7 6 5 4 3 2
A Pied Piper Book is a registered trademark of
Dial Books for Young Readers,
a division of NAL Penguin Inc.,
® TM 1,163,686 and ® TM 1,054,312.

A DARK DARK TALE
is published in a hardcover edition by
Dial Books for Young Readers.
ISBN 0-8037-0093-8

The art consists of acrylic paintings that are
color-separated and reproduced in full color.

A DARK DARK TALE

Story and pictures by

RUTH BROWN

Dial Books for Young Readers

New York

Once upon a time there
was a dark, dark moor.

On the moor there was
a dark, dark wood.

In the wood there was
a dark, dark house.

At the front of the house
there was a dark, dark door.

Behind the door there
was a dark, dark hall.

In the hall there were
some dark, dark stairs.

Up the stairs there was
a dark, dark passage.

**Across the passage was
a dark, dark curtain.**

Behind the curtain was
a dark, dark room.

In the room was a dark,
dark cupboard.

In the cupboard was
a dark, dark corner.

In the corner was
a dark, dark box.

And in the box there was... A MOUSE!